"There is nothing permanent except change."
—Heraclitus

To my nephew Bernardo. And everyone who, at some point in their lives, felt like a fish out of water. Thanks to Heather, Kelsey, Merideth, Teresa, Theo, and Ricardo.

Text and illustrations copyright © 2018 by Vin Vogel
All rights reserved. No part of this book may be reproduced, or stored in a retrieval system, or transmitted in any form or by any means, electronic, mechanical, photocopying, recording, or otherwise, without express written permission of the publisher. Published by Two Lions, New York
www.apub.com

Amazon, the Amazon logo, and Two Lions are trademarks of Amazon.com, Inc., or its affiliates.
ISBN-13: 9781503902602 ISBN-10: 1503902609
The illustrations are rendered in digital media.
Book design by AndWorld Design. Printed in China. First Edition
13 5 7 9 10 8 6 4 2

A HOME
FOR LEO

two lions

GOO!

BRRRR

ARK-ARK?

ARK

Leo grew up in the sea.

It was different
from his old life.

But he had a **family** he loved.

Leo was happy.

He was **different** from the other creatures, though.

He couldn't hold his breath underwater for as long as they could.

And he didn't **look** like anyone else.

Sometimes he felt like an empty shell.

One day, he met a creature who looked like him.

And **everything** changed.

Leo was like a fish out of water . . .

. . . until his parents recognized him on TV.

He recognized them right back.

Leo was happy again.

Even if there was a **LOT** to adjust to.

Hi!

ARK! ARK!

Leo loved his parents and his new life,
but he missed his other family . . .

. . . and the sea.

He longed to play
in the waves and sleep
under a wide-open,
starry sky.

His parents tried to help . . .

. . . but sometimes he STILL
felt a bit like an empty shell.

Leo thought about what to do.

Nothing made sense.

Until **something** did. Even the cat thought so.

Now **everyone** was happy.

Most of all, Leo.